Move your feet!
Oh!
VRRRR
VRRRR
VRRRR
VRRRR
....partly cloudy with a chance of...
Relax dude. It's your Dad coming, not the Pope.
I wouldn't vacuum for the Pope.
I thought he retired?
SNORT
My dad's just been having a hard time after losing his job.
Yeah, that's what he's telling everyone.
He actually got let go, after 25 years. Kinda hurt his pride.
He's been struggling to find a new job-
but he doesn't want anyone to know, so don't say anything!
My lips are sealed.
I0714502

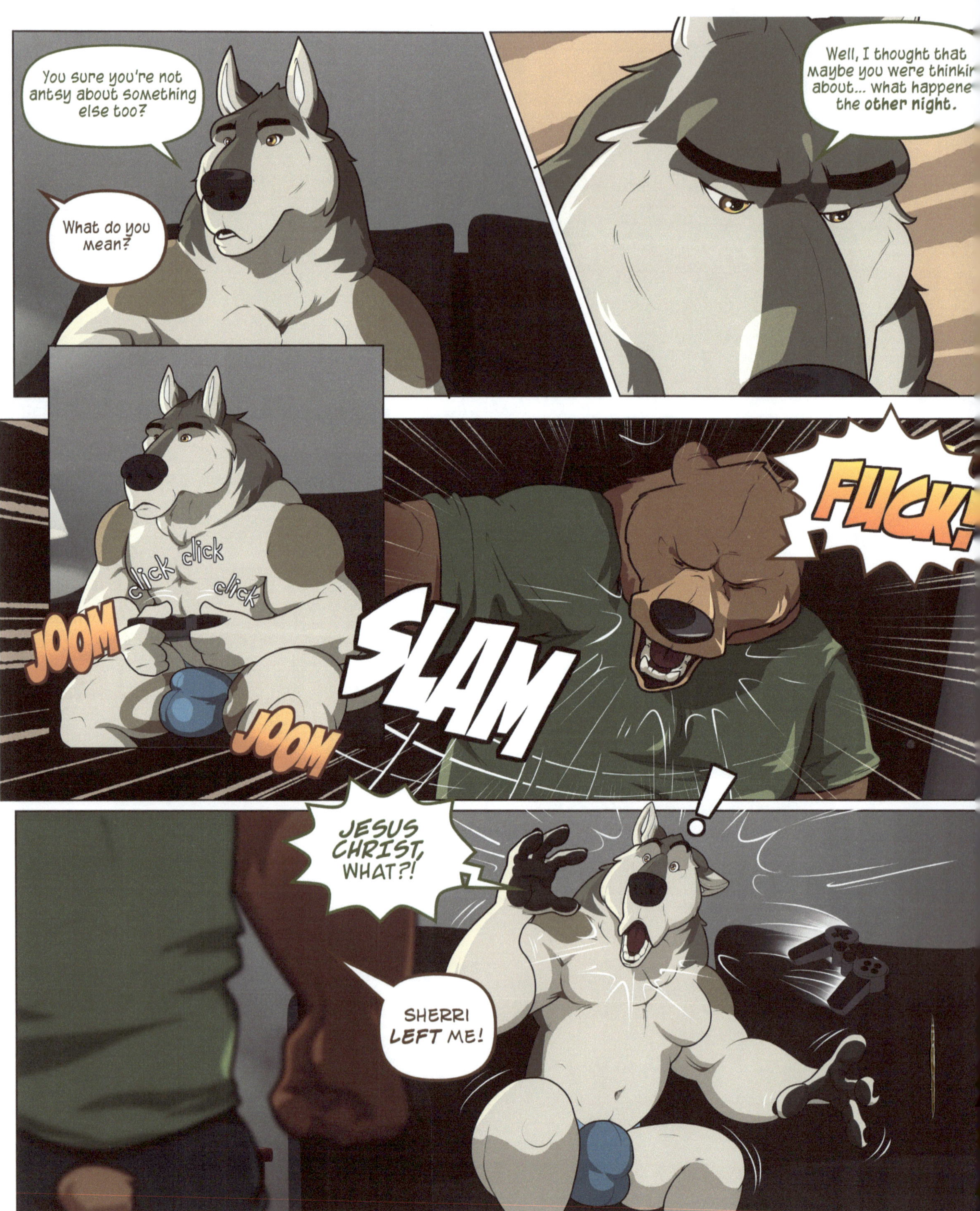

You sure you're not antsy about something else too?
What do you mean?
Well, I thought that maybe you were thinkir about... what happene the other night.
click click click
JOOM
JOOM
SLAM
FUCK!
JESUS CHRIST, WHAT?!
SHERRI LEFT ME!

Shit, I'm sorry man. What happened?
We haven't done it for WEEKS! OF COURSE it's all I'm thinking about!
I tried to get a little nookie, she said that's ALL I think about and said she was tired of it!
Damn straight!
It sucks that she broke up with you over that.
Snort Shit. Maybe.
I was SO looking forward to it too. So pent up.
But if she never wants it when you do... that's not gonna work out well in the end.
...Pent up, huh?

Dude, I appreciate the occasional blow, but...
Not tonight. Don't know if you could handle my mood right now.
Well, maybe it's not my mouth that would be handling it?
Heh?
FUCK!
Nng!
hah!
snort
yeah
right there
Ugh
ooh
mmf
SHLP
FFP
PLAP
PLP
PLAP
SMAK
SHLP!

BACK IN THE PRESENT...
No. Why do you ask?
Well... that was just a new thing for you and I was a little worried-
We're good, dude.
...okay.
Fuck, is he here already? He wasn't supposed to arrive 'till 6!
KNOCK KNOCK
I'll get it.
DO NOT OPEN THE DOOR IN YOUR JOCKSTRAP!
Jesus, fine! It's probably just the postman anyway!
Hi. You must be Calvin's dad.
Sorry I'm not dressed. Calvin thought you'd be here later.
Yes-
oh
Ne worry Lad! I spent many a weekend in my boxers 'till it was time to hit the town!
I'm Sid.

Come on in. I'll just go and throw something more appropriate on.
No need to stand on ceremony on my account. I'm just an old mechanic, not the feckin' queen!
Hi Dad!
I'm just glad you're letting an old fart like me invade your space for so long!

I'll just be a minute!
whatever!

A MINUTE LATER
Hey Ardent, fancy a cuppa?
Coffee please.
I'll have to make some.

So, what are your plans for the day?
After tea I thought I'd take Dad to see the castle on the hill, then maybe a meal in town. Sound good, Dad?
Whatever is good with you! I'm just happy to spend some time with my son - haven't seen you in six months!

How about you, Ar? Want to tag along?

Nah, I've seen those sights already. I wouldn't want to be in the way.
Was planning on going out on the town later.
Young stud out on the prowl, eh?
DAD!
Hey, I remember when I was young I was always out on the prowl - before I met your mum!
Only natural for a guy to go looking for a gir-
- a partner. Assuming he doesn't have one?
Nah, no boyfriend at the moment.
So it's just blokes you're interested in?
DAD!
I'm gay, so just blokes. But never say never I suppose. I've been with a few 'straight' guys before.
Feckin' hell, Calvin, I'm just askin' the question!

See? He don' take offense. Cal here don' trust me not to embarrass him.
grumble

Well, okay, we should be going.
DING DING

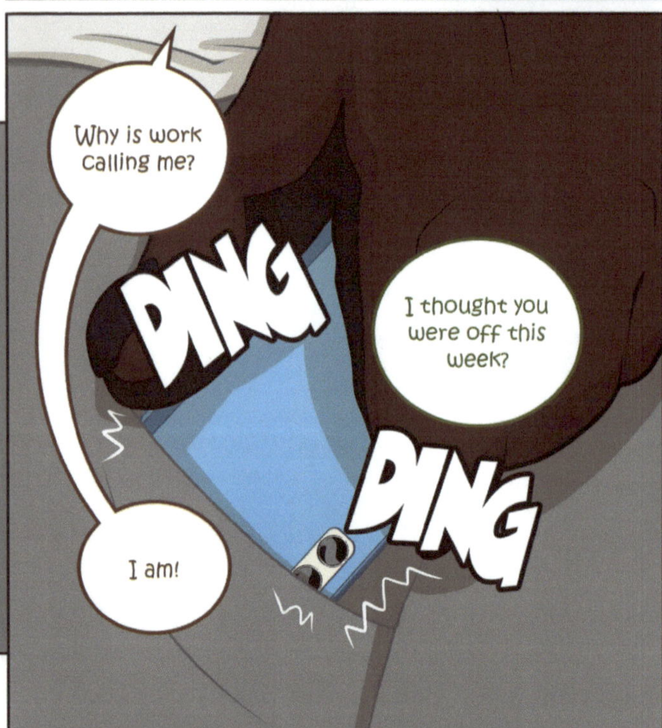

Why is work calling me?
I thought you were off this week?
I am!
DING
DING

I'll be just a minute. Hello?

Sorry if I made yeh uncomfortable, lad. I know I'm not as modern as I think I am sometimes.
Ha. You're light-years ahead of my father, if that helps!
WELL FUCK!

Total incompetent ARSEHOLES, the lot of them!

What's up?

They didn't record my day off for today!

Plus a couple nurses in the ER called in sick so they need me to help cover. I'm sorry, Ar, could you - ?

You want ME to show him the sights?

Don't be stupid. Just hang out here for the day. Rent a movie or something.

Uh, you know I'm housebroken right?

Fine, but we're ordering a shit-ton of sushi.

AND IF HE WETS HIMSELF, I'M NOT CHANGING HIM!
YOU KNOW, I CAN HANDLE BEING HERE BY MYSELF. I DON' WANT TO SPOIL YER EVENING.
DON'T WORRY ABOUT IT. THERE'S OTHER NIGHTS!
I'LL CALL IN FOR THE SUSHI WHILE YOU PICK OUT WHAT TO WATCH.
HAR HAR

LATER

I HAVE NO IDEA HOW HE'S KEEPING A STRAIGHT FACE.
BECAUSE YOU'RE NOT MR. BENSENMUM... YOU'RE HIS DAUGHTER!

I USED TO GO TO FLICKS LIKE THIS WITH MY WIFE. WHEN SHE WAS GONE... IT'S NOT THE SAME GOING ALONE, YOU KNOW?

I GET THAT. WANNA PUT ON ANOTHER?
I'M GOOD. ANYWAY, YOU WERE PLANNING TO GO OUT. SERIOUSLY, DON'T LET ME STOP YOU.

I PROMISED CAL I'D STAY. BESIDES, IT'S NOT BEEN A BAD EVENING.
I CAN ALWAYS FIND SOMEONE ON AN APP TOMORROW AND SEE HOW IT GOES.
PLUS, FOR A YOUNG HEALTHY UN LIKE YOURSELF EVERYBODY'S SWIPING LEFT OR RIGHT.
OR WHATEVER MEANS ' I WANNA TAKE YOU TO BONE TOWN.'
BONE TOWN?!
AH. NEVER GOT THE HANG OF THOSE THINGS. NEVER KNEW WHICH WAY TO SWIPE.
PLUS THOSE OLDER BIRDS ARE PRETTY RESERVED. NONE OF 'EM HOLD A CANDLE TO MY DEAR MARY.
BONE TOWN, POUND TOWN, WHATEVER YOU YOUNG GUYS CALL DIPPING YOUR WICK!
HA HA HA HA HA
I DO ALL RIGHT. PLENTY OF FUN AND EVEN MADE A LITTLE CASH.

THEY PAY? DIDN'T THINK YOU WERE THE TYPE TO GO THAT ROUTE.
NOT EXACTLY. THEY DON'T PAY. WE KINDA... BOTH MAKE SOME CASH.
NOT SURE I FOLLOW.
YOU KNOW WHAT LIVE-STREAMING IS?
OH. YEAH. I THINK SO.
WELL, IF A GUY IS UP FOR IT WE... PUT UP A WEBCAM AND PEOPLE PAY US TO - ERM- DO CERTAIN THINGS.
AH.
MAKE MUCH MONEY FROM IT?
SOMETIMES. DEPENDS. LAST WEEK I MADE £350 FOR A COUPLE BLOWS AND A... KNOTTING. HEH.
£350 IN ONE NIGHT AND YOU GOT TO HAVE SEX. PRETTY SWEET DEAL!
PITY THERE AIN'T A MARKET FOR FAT OLD GUYS LIKE ME, I COULD USE THAT KIND OF EARNING POWER!

AND THE WHOLE STRAIGHT-TO-GAY THING IS A BIG TURN ON FOR A LOT OF GUYS.
ESPECIALLY IF IT'S... YOUR FIRST TIME.
WELL... ACTUALLY GAY GUYS REALLY, UM, LIKE OLDER GUYS.
PAY ME EXTRA TO CALL THEM DADDY.
FUCK FUCK FUCK FUCK FUCK FUCK FUCK FUCK FUCK FUCK FUCK FUCK FUCK FUCK FUCK FUCK FUCK FUCK FUCK FUCK FUCK FUCK FUCK FUCK FUCK
WELL, UH, WHAT WOULD I HAVE TO DO?
ONLY WHAT YOU'RE WILLING TO DO. COULD JUST BE A HANDJOB, OR BLOWJOB.
BUT YOU'RE BOUND TO GET MORE IF YOU GO FARTHER.
YEAH?
WE COULD SET UP SOME GOALS BEFOREHAND, SAY £200 AND I BLOW YOU.

WELL ALL RIGHT THEN, IF YOU THINK THEY'D PAY TO SEE A GUY LIKE ME. I AIN'T PRECIOUS AND COULD USE THE CASH.
OH — OKAY! RIGHT NOW?
SURE, NO TIME LIKE THE PRESENT!
3:21
Cancel
Public
Hey everybody! I've got a DILF daddy bd
Tweet
TAP
TAP
TAP
TAP
I'M JUST GONNA LET PEOPLE KNOW WHAT'S GOING ON.
GET THEM EXCITED ABOUT COMING INTO THE STREAM.
KAY — DO I NEED TO... GET DRESSED UP OR SOMETHING?
QUITE THE OPPOSITE. THEY'RE GONNA WANT TO SEE THAT DADDY BEAR BODY.
'DADDY BEAR?'
I MEAN, I'M A BEAR WHO'S A DAD, BUT —
I'VE GOT A JOCK YOU CAN WEAR. FOLLOW ME BACK HERE.

LEMME FIND IT... HERE.
IS IT OK IF I CALL YOU DADDY DURING THE STREAM?
DADDY'S FINE.

HERE YOU GO.
KINDA SMALL, ISN'T IT?
KINDA THE POINT.

TOO BAD WE DON'T HAVE A CAMERAMAN. BETTER ANGLES, EXTRA COCK, EXTRA TIPS!
PITY WE CAN'T ASK CAL. IF ONLY TO WATCH HIS HEAD EXPLODE.
KLAK
KLAK
KLAK
KLAK
KLAK
KLAK

WILL THIS DO?

OH. UHH...

YEAH... YEAH THAT'S GREAT.
UM, WE'RE NOT TELLING CAL ABOUT THIS, ARE WE?
SURE! I'LL ALSO TELL HIM ABOUT THE NIGHT KNOCKED UP HIS MUM!
SO, YOU UH, GETTING EXCITED THEN?
EASY LAD, DON'T GIVE IT AWAY FOR FREE!
FINE, LET'S SET UP SOME DONATION GOALS.
LATER...
SO, LET'S TALK FUCKING?
£400 FOR ME TO FUCK YOU AND... IS £800 TOO MUCH FOR YOU TO TOP?
GASP UH – NO, THAT'S FINE.
tap
tap
tap
tap
HOW MUCH FOR... THE KNOT? THEY TEND TO PAY WELL FOR THAT.
EXTRA GRAND AND I TAKE THE KNOT. SOUND GOOD?
YOU'RE REMARKABLY COOL ABOUT THIS.
HEH. WHEN I DECIDE TO DO SOMETHING I FIGURE, GO ALL THE WAY.

OK, THAT'S ENOUGH GOALS. THEY'LL PROBABLY ASK FOR A FEW THINGS, BUT IF YOU'RE NOT UP FOR IT JUST SAY NO.
CLICK
OH, DON'T WORRY LAD. I KNOW WHEN TO SAY NO. WHAT SHOULD I BE DOING?
JUST STAND THERE WHILE I GET IT STARTED. PEOPLE WILL ENJOY THE VIEW.
GO LIVE

kegelmaster: FIRST
penishead: first!
penishead: fuck.
dingbat234: Hey cuties
cockdude: I SEE A BULGE
26
HEY GUYS! I TOLD YOU I HAD A SPECIAL TREAT. THIS IS MY ROOMMATE'S DAD, BUT TONIGHT I'M CALLING HIM DADDY!
SAY HI.

cockdude: I SEE A BULGE
feral: sup losers
ballboy: Is that a bear??
penishead: I wanted to be first...
porno207king: belly
42
OH SHITE YOU MEANT ME. ER, HI GUYS. I'M SID. OR DADDY, WHATEVER.

THEY HAVE SOME QUESTIONS. CARE FOR SOME Q AND A BEFORE THE 'D' AND 'A?'
ER, SURE, I GUESS!
THEY WANT TO KNOW IF YOU'RE REALLY MY ROOMMATE'S DAD. HEY, I SAID HE WAS!
YEAH, I JUST MET HIM TODAY. IN TOWN VISITING MY SON AND HE HAD TO GO TO WORK.
A FEW BEERS LATER AND HERE WE ARE, HEH!
crik
OH, AND TO GUESS YOUR NEXT QUESTION, YES I'M STRAIGHT. MARRIED FOR 25 YEARS AND NEVER LOOKED AT A BLOKE BEFORE TONIGHT.
GOOD GUESS. UM, THEY'RE WONDERING WHERE SHE IS?
AH — I'M A WIDOWER. AIN'T HAD NOTHING BUT MY OWN HAND FOR COMPANY FOR A FEW YEARS.
ONE GUY IS ASKING HOW BIG YOUR BALLS ARE.
IS THAT TOO MUCH?

WELL, GIVE 'EM A FUMBLE AND SEE WHAT YA THINK!
nudge
WOW.
AYE LAD. YOU DON'T GET MANY OF THEM FRUITS TO THE POUND.
SNRK

ALL RIGHT, I HAVE CHAT ON MY PHONE BUT AS YOU CAN SEE I'M GONNA HAVE MY HANDS VERY FULL.
heh
jiggle
HMMM!
FIRST GAY KISS AND A LITTLE STROKING. YOU OK TO START?
READY AND ABLE. NOW, LESS TALKING AND MORE KISSING. DON'T BE GENTLE, SON.

SLP
SMAK
MMF
HMM
HNG
AH
HMF
HNG
AH
SQUEEZE
GROPE
HMF
MMF

heh
plap
FUCK!
amarutha: DO IT
penisbutt: omg that dick
Gayfatbuoy: SUCK COCK
IF YOU WANT A
TASTE, I THINK WE
HIT THAT GOAL!

YES DADDY.
mnrg~
slurp
SLK
mmf
FP SHLD
hah
woof
hnng
HNNG. WOW.

DING
DING DING
SHLP
MMF
SMK
SLRP
NOPE, NOT GONNA COMPARE HIM WITH MY WIFE.
HI AGAIN! FUCK, IT'S GOOD SO FAR!
BUT BETTER THAN MOST OTHER GIRLS I DIPPED MY WICK IN!
SLK
SHP
MMF
SLRP
THAT'S A GOOD BOY. NICE AND DEEP, SON.
SQUEEZE
DAMN, YOU GUYS MIND IF I JUST FUCK HIS MUZZLE?
I AIN'T GONNA LAST MUCH LONGER WITH HOW GOOD HE HIS!
!

FUCK YEAH. THAT'S THE SHIT.
SMAK
mmf
SHLP
FFP
PLAP
SLP
FP
HUMP
SMAK
SMAK
PLAP
SHP
SLK
FFP
SHLP
FUCK! ANY SECOND NOW, SON!
SMAK
FFP
SHLP

OH FUCK, FUCK, FUCK!
SO, FIRST MUZZLE JOB FROM A GUY!
WHAT DO YOU THINK
sploot
lick
DADDY APPROVES! HEH. WHOO.
OH.
HEY, WE'VE MET OUR NEXT GOAL!
DADDY GETS TO TASTE COCK FOR THE FIRST TIME!
DING!

WHEN IN ROME, I GUESS!
OH!
SCHLP!
DADDY!
SLK
SHLP
MMH
SLK
SLP
FFP
SLK
FMP
SLK
SHLP
MHM
SLK
SHLK

OH — I'M CLOSE ALREADY!
ALL RIGHT GUYS, IF YOU WANT ME TO SWALLOW TIP £20 AND I'LL SUCK THIS WOLF BONE DRY!
squeeze
DING
DING DING
DING
DING
DING
THANKS LADS!
AGH!
SCHLOMP

sploot
NNG!
BLEH. ACQUIRED TASTE.
OH - D'YEH THINK WE MADE THE NEXT GOAL?
I DON'T FUCKING CARE, JUST LUBE UP AND FUCK ME ALREADY.
ER- ALRIGHT. WHERE DO YOU KEEP IT?
ON THE DRESSER!
Squirt
SLK
SLK
SLK
SLK
SLK

ding
WELL YOU MIGHT NOT CARE SON, BUT LOOKS LIKE AFTER THIS I'LL BE TAKING YER KNOT.
SO DON'T BLOW ANOTHER LOAD WHILE I HAS YOUR TAIL!
!
!
!
!
YOU WANT ME TO GO SLOW, SON?
UGH...
ffp
NO FUCKING WAY DADDY, FUCK ME AS HARD AS YOU CAN.
FUUUCK! YOU TAKE COCK LIKE A CHAMP, EH?
shlp!

AH
YIP
SLP
FFP
SLP
SMAK
SMAK
grunt
fuck!
UGH
FUCK
AH
SLP
HUMP
PLAP
FFP
MMG! FUCK!

SLAP
FFP
SMAK
SLP
FFP
SMK
SLP

OH YES!
SLP FFP PLAP HUMP
HUMP PLAP HUMP
PLAP HUMP FFP
HUMP SSHP FFP
OAGH
throb
throb
Sploot

SMAK!
ALL RIGHT SON, THAT WAS REALLY NICE.
NOW I GUESS IT'S MY TURN, SO UP ON YER FEET!
I'LL TAKE IT SLOW, ALL RIGHT?
HEH! I'M NOT SOME DELICATE FLOWER!
slk
slk
slk
FUCK YEAH!
DADDY'S BEEN AROUND THE BLOCK AND BACK. SO STICK IT IN ME AND HAVE FUN!

GASP
FFP
NNG!
SORRY! NEED A SEC?
ALL THE WAY TO MY KNOT, DADDY!
JUST A A MOMENT. DAMN SON, YOU'RE BIGGER THAN YOU LOOK!
HRRRGH...
HAHAHAHA!

HOW'S IT FEEL?
FINE SO FAR. 'AVE AT IT, SON!
plap
ffp
plap
hump
ffp
hah
grunt
DADDY LIKING IT?
hump
FFP
plap
AH... AIN'T DISLIKING IT!
YOU CAN GO FASTER, SON... IF YOU WANT TO.

THANK YOU, DADDY!
ffp
SQUEEZE
smak
ffp
plop
ffp
smak
plap
DING
DING
DING
DING
DING
DING
HOLY S...
Shove tha... in!!
...e it easy on the virgin!!
hah
grunt

smak
plap
hump
plap
ffp smak
GRIND
FUCK - AH -
GO ON,
SON.
OH
GOD!
OOH!!
FFFFFP
plop

SHIT!
ffp
hump
NNG!
plap
plap
hump hump
plap ffp
hump
hump
OH FUCK!
FUCK!
RAAAGH!
OH GOD!
huff
hah
hah
hah
hah
FUCK SON, THAT'S A DAMN BIG KNOT! HOW LONG...?
HUFF ABOUT HALF AN HOUR.

cockdude: my keyboard is ruined.
quaddum: sup losers
penishead: damn that knot must feel good.
horselover1996: fuck
quickie22: this ain't coming out of my fur.
WELL GUYS, I HOPE YOU ENJOYED AS MUCH AS WE HAVE!
WE'RE GONNA BE HERE A WHILE, SO I'M GONNA END THE STREAM.
SID, ANY THOUGHTS ON YOUR FIRST TIME WITH A GUY?
YA KNOW, IT WAS A LOT OF FUN! BUT I WON'T BE ABLE TO RIDE A BIKE FOR A MONTH!
I'LL BE HERE ALL WEEK! TIP YOUR WAITERS!
BOOP!
WELL THAT WAS... A UNIQUE WAY OF ENDING IT!
THE HELL SHOULD I KNOW HOW TO END IT?
I GOTTA SAY, I DID NOT EXPECT YOU TO TAKE MY KNOT UP YOUR ASS SO EASILY!
smack
SO I'M NOT YOUR FIRST?!
WELL, I DIDN'T TELL YEH – IT'S TRUE I AIN'T BEEN WITH A GUY, BUT ME AN' THE WIFE... YOU KNOW WHAT PEGGING IS?
WELL, YOU'RE THE FIRST THAT'S NOT MADE O' RUBBER!

DAMN, I DUNNO IF MY LEGS CAN KEEP ME UP LIKE THIS FOR 30 MINUTES. MIND IF I LEAN ON YA?
LADS, I'M HOME FINALLY!
DID YOU FIND SOMETHING TO—
WHAT ELSE IS ALL THAT PADDING FOR?
OH MY GOD!
I... DON'T EVEN WANT TO KNOW.
SLAM